The Original Adventures of
Raggedy Ann
and
Raggedy Andy

The Original Adventures of
Raggedy Ann
and
Raggedy Andy

Johnny Gruelle

DERRYDALE BOOKS
New York

This 1991 edition is published by Derrydale Books, distributed by Outlet Book Company, Inc., a Random House Company, 225 Park Avenue South, New York, New York 10003, by arrangement with Macmillan, Inc.

Printed and bound in the United States of America

Library of Congress Cataloging-in-Publication Data
Gruelle, Johnny, 1880?-1939.
   [Raggedy Ann stories]
   The original adventures of Raggedy Ann and Raggedy Andy / Johnny Gurelle.
      p.   cm.
   Summary: A collection of adventures featuring the well-known red-haired dolls Raggedy Ann and Raggedy Andy.
   ISBN 0-517-06631-9
   [1. Dolls—Fiction.] I. Gruelle, Johnny, 1880?-1938. Raggedy Andy stories. 1992. II. Title.
PZ7.G9324Rag 1992
[E]—dc20
                                             91-28815
                                             CIP
                                             AC

Cover design by Clair Moritz

The Original Adventures of
Raggedy Ann

PREFACE AND DEDICATION

AS I write this, I have before me on my desk, propped up against the telephone, an old rag doll. Dear old Raggedy Ann!

The same Raggedy Ann with which my mother played when a child.

There she sits, a trifle loppy and loose-jointed, looking me squarely in the face in a straightforward, honest manner, a twinkle where her shoe-button eyes reflect the light.

Evidently Raggedy has been to a tea party today, for her face is covered with chocolate.

She smiles happily and continuously.

True, she has been nibbled by mice, who have made nests out of the soft cotton with which she has been stuffed, but Raggedy smiled just as broadly when the mice nibbled at her, for her smile is painted on.

What adventures you must have had, Raggedy!

What joy and happiness you have brought into this world!

And no matter what treatment you have received, how patient you have been!

What lessons of kindness and fortitude you might teach could you but talk; you with your wisdom of seventy years. No wonder rag dolls are the best beloved! You are so kindly, so patient, so lovable.

The more you become torn, tattered and loose-jointed, rag dolls, the more you are loved by children.

Who knows but that Fairyland is filled with old, lovable rag dolls—soft, loppy rag dolls who ride through all the wonders of Fairyland in the crook of dimpled arms, snuggling close to childish breasts within which beat hearts filled with eternal sunshine.

So, to the millions of children and grown-ups who have loved a rag doll, I dedicate these stories of Raggedy Ann.

JOHNNY GRUELLE

INTRODUCTION

MARCELLA liked to play up in the attic at Grandma's quaint old house, way out in the country, for there were so many old forgotten things to find up there.

One day when Marcella was up in the attic and had played with the old spinning wheel until she had grown tired of it, she curled up on an old horse-hair sofa to rest.

"I wonder what is in that barrel, way back in the corner?" she thought, as she jumped from the sofa and climbed over two dusty trunks to the barrel standing back under the eaves.

It was quite dark back there, so when Marcella had pulled a large bundle of things from the barrel she took them over to the dormer window where she could see better. There was a funny little bonnet with long white ribbons. Marcella put it on.

In an old leather bag she found a number of tintypes of queer-looking men and women in old-fashioned clothes. And there was one picture of a very pretty little girl with long curls tied tightly back from her forehead and wearing a long dress and queer pantaloons that reached to her shoe tops. And then out of the heap she pulled an old rag doll with only one shoe-button eye and a painted nose and a smiling mouth. Her dress was of soft material, blue with pretty little flowers and dots all over it.

Forgetting everything else in the happiness of her find, Marcella caught up the rag doll and ran downstairs to show it to Grandma.

"Well! Well! Where did you find it?" Grandma cried. "It's old Raggedy Ann!" she went on as she hugged the doll to her breast. "I had forgotten her. She has been in the attic for sixty-one years, I guess! Well! Well! Well! Dear old Raggedy Ann! I will sew another button on her right away!" and Grandma went to the machine drawer and got her needle and thread.

Marcella watched the sewing while Grandma told how she had played with Raggedy Ann when she was a little girl.

"Now!" Grandma laughed, "Raggedy Ann, you have two fine shoe-button eyes and with them you can see the changes that have taken place in the world while you have been shut up so long in the attic! For, Raggedy Ann, you have a new playmate and mistress now, and I hope you both will have as much happiness together as you and I used to have!"

Then Grandma gave Raggedy Ann to Marcella, saying very seriously, "Marcella, let me introduce my very dear friend, Raggedy Ann. Raggedy, this is my grand-daughter, Marcella!" And Grandma gave the doll a twitch with her fingers in such a way that the rag doll nodded her head to Marcella.

"Oh, Grandma! Thank you ever and ever so much!" Marcella cried as she gave Grandma a hug and kiss. "Raggedy Ann and I will have just loads of fun."

And this is how Raggedy Ann joined the doll family at Marcella's house, where she began the adventures of Raggedy Ann, told in the following stories.

RAGGEDY ANN LEARNS A LESSON

ONE DAY the dolls were left all to themselves.

Their little mistress had placed them all around the room and told them to be nice children while she was away.

And there they sat and never even so much as wiggled a finger, until their mistress had left the room.

Then the soldier dolly turned his head and solemnly winked at Raggedy Ann.

And when the front gate clicked and the dollies knew they were alone, they all scrambled to their feet.

"Now let's have a good time!" cried the tin soldier. "Let's all go in search of something to eat!"

"Yes! Let's all go in search of something to eat!" cried all the other dollies.

"When Mistress had me out playing this morning," said Raggedy Ann, "she carried me by a door near the back of the house and I smelled something that smelled as if it would taste delicious!"

"Then you lead the way, Raggedy Ann!" cried the French dolly.

"I think it would be a good plan to elect Raggedy Ann as our leader on this expedition!" said the Indian doll.

1

At this all the other dolls clapped their hands together and shouted, "Hurrah! Raggedy Ann will be our leader."

So Raggedy Ann, very proud indeed to have the confidence and love of the other dollies, said that she would be very glad to be their leader.

"Follow me!" she cried as her wobbly legs carried her across the floor at a lively pace.

The other dollies followed, racing about the house until they came to the pantry door. "This is the place!" cried Raggedy Ann, and sure enough, all the dollies smelled something that they knew must be very good to eat.

But none of the dollies was tall enough to open the door and, although they pushed and pulled with all their might, the door remained tightly closed.

The dollies were talking and pulling and pushing and every once in a while one would fall over and the others would step on her in their efforts to open the door. Finally Raggedy Ann drew away and sat down on the floor.

When the other dollies discovered Raggedy Ann sitting there, running her rag hands through her yarn hair, they knew she was thinking.

"Shhh!" they said to each other and quietly went over near Raggedy Ann and sat down in front of her.

"There must be a way!" said Raggedy Ann.

"Raggedy says there must be a way to get inside!" cried all the dolls.

"I can't seem to think clearly today," said Raggedy Ann. "It feels as if my head were ripped."

At this the French doll ran to Raggedy Ann and took off her bonnet. "Yes, there is a rip in your head, Raggedy!" she said, and she pulled a pin from her skirt and pinned up Raggedy's head. "It's not a very neat job, for I got some puckers in it!" she said.

"Oh, that is ever so much better!" cried Raggedy Ann. "Now I can think quite clearly."

"Now Raggedy can think clearly!" cried all the dolls.

"My thoughts must have leaked out the rip before!" said Raggedy Ann.

"They must have leaked out before, dear Raggedy!" cried all the other dolls.

"Now that I can think so clearly," said Raggedy Ann, "I think the door must be locked and to get in we must unlock it!"

"That will be easy," said the Dutch doll who says "Mama" when he is tipped backward and forward, "for the brave tin soldier can shoot the key out of the lock!"

"I can easily do that!" cried the tin soldier, as he raised his gun.

"Oh, Raggedy Ann!" cried the French dolly. "Please do not let him shoot!"

"No!" said Raggedy Ann. "We must think of a quieter way!"

After thinking quite hard for a moment, Raggedy Ann jumped up and said, "I have it!" And she caught up the jumping jack and held him up to the door; then Jack slid up his stick and unlocked the door.

Then the dollies all pushed and the door swung open.

My! Such a scramble! The dolls piled over one another in their desire to be the first at the goodies.

They swarmed upon the pantry shelves and in their eagerness spilled a pitcher of cream, which ran all over the French dolly's dress.

The Indian doll found some corn bread and, dipping it in the molasses, he sat down for a good feast.

A jar of raspberry jam was overturned and the dollies ate this until their faces were all purple.

The tin soldier fell from the shelf three times and bent one of his tin legs, but he scrambled right back up again.

Never had the dolls had so much fun and excitement! They had all eaten their fill when they heard the click of the front gate.

They did not take time to climb from the shelves, but all rolled or jumped off to the floor and scrambled back to

5

their room as fast as they could run, leaving a trail of bread crumbs and jam along the way back to the nursery.

Just as their mistress came into the room the dolls dropped in whatever positions they happened to be in.

"This is funny!" cried Mistress. "They were all left sitting in their places around the room! I wonder if Fido has been shaking them up!" Then she saw Raggedy Ann's face and picked her up. "Why Raggedy Ann, you are all sticky! I do believe you are covered with jam!" and Mistress tasted Raggedy Ann's hand. "Yes! It's JAM! Shame on you, Raggedy Ann! You've been in the pantry and all the others, too!" And with this the dolls' mistress dropped Raggedy Ann on the floor and left the room.

When she came back she had on an apron and her sleeves were rolled up.

She picked up all the sticky dolls and putting them in a basket she carried them out under the apple tree in the garden.

There she had placed her little tub and wringer and she took the dolls, one at a time, and scrubbed them with a scrubbing brush and soused them up and down and this way and that in the soapsuds until they were clean.

Then she hung them all out on the clothesline in the sunshine to dry.

There the dolls hung all day, swinging and twisting about as the breeze swayed the clothesline.

"I do believe she scrubbed my face so hard she wore off my smile!" said Raggedy Ann, after an hour of silence.

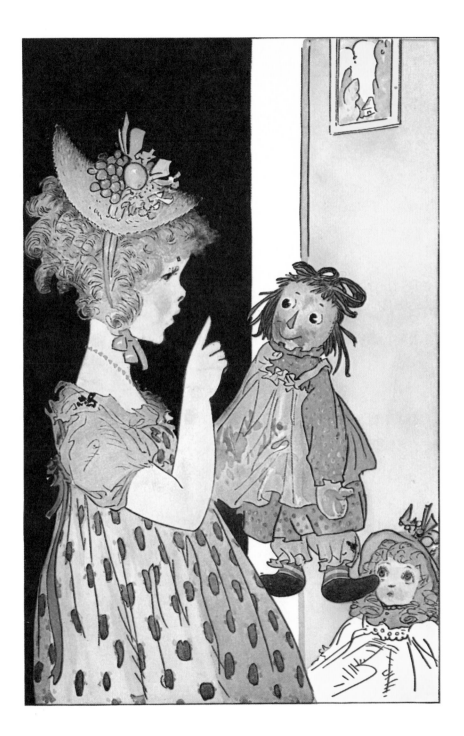

"No, it is still there!" said the tin soldier, as the wind twisted him around so he could see Raggedy. "But I do believe my arms will never work without squeaking, they feel so rusted," he added.

Just then the wind twisted the little Dutch doll and loosened his clothespin, so that he fell to the grass below with a sawdusty bump, and as he rolled over he said, "Mama!" in a squeaky voice.

Late in the afternoon the back door opened and the little mistress came out with a table and chairs. After setting the table she took all the dolls from the line and placed them about the table.

They had lemonade with grape jelly in it, which made it a beautiful lavender color, and little "Baby-teeny-weeny-cookies" with powdered sugar on them.

After this lovely dinner, the dollies were taken in the house, where they had their hair brushed and nice clean nighties put on.

Then they were placed in their beds and Mistress kissed each one good night and tiptoed from the room, closing the door very gently behind her.

All the dolls lay as still as mice for a few minutes, then Raggedy Ann raised up on her cotton-stuffed elbows and said: "I have been thinking!"

"Sh!" said all the other dollies. "Raggedy has been thinking!"

"Yes," said Raggedy Ann, "I have been thinking; our mistress gave us the nice dinner out under the trees to teach us a lesson. She wanted to teach us that we could have had all the goodies we wished if we had behaved ourselves. And our lesson was that we must never take without asking what we could always have for the asking! So let us all remember and try never again to do anything that might cause those who love us any unhappiness of any kind!"

"Let us all remember," chimed all the other dollies.

And Raggedy Ann, with a merry twinkle in her shoe-button eyes, lay back in her little bed, her cotton head filled with thoughts of love and happiness.

RAGGEDY ANN AND THE KITE

RAGGEDY ANN watched the preparations with great interest.

A number of sticks were being fastened together with strings and covered with light cloth.

Raggedy Ann heard some of the boys talk of "The Kite," so Raggedy Ann knew this must be a kite.

When a tail had been fastened to the kite and a large ball of heavy twine tied to the front, one of the boys held the kite up in the air and another boy walked off, unwinding the ball of twine.

There was a nice breeze blowing, so the boy with the twine called, "Let 'er go!" and started running.

Marcella held Raggedy up so that she could watch.

How nicely it climbed! But suddenly the kite acted strangely, and as all the children shouted advice to the boy with the ball of twine, the kite began darting this way and that, and finally making four or five loop-the-loops, it crashed to the ground.

"It needs more tail on it!" one boy shouted.

Then the children asked each other where they might get more rags to fasten to the tail of the kite.

"Let's tie Raggedy Ann to the tail!" suggested Marcella. "I know she would enjoy a trip way up in the sky!"

The boys all shouted with delight at this new suggestion. So Raggedy Ann was tied to the tail of the kite.

This time the kite rose straight in the air and remained steady. The ball of twine unwound until the kite and Raggedy Ann were way, way up and far away. How Raggedy Ann enjoyed being up there! She could see for miles and miles! And how tiny the children looked!

Suddenly a great puff of wind came and carried Raggedy Ann streaming way out behind the kite! She could hear the wind singing on the twine as the strain increased.

Suddenly Raggedy Ann felt something rip. It was the rag to which she was tied. As each puff of wind caught her the rip widened.

When Marcella watched Raggedy Ann rise high above the field, she wondered how much Raggedy Ann enjoyed it, and wished that she, too, might have gone along. But after the kite had been up in the air for five or ten minutes, Marcella grew restless. Kites were rather tiresome. There was more fun in tea parties out under the apple tree.

"Will you please pull down the kite now?" she asked the boy with the twine. "I want Raggedy Ann."

"Let her ride up there!" the boy replied. "We'll bring her home when we pull down the kite! We're going to get another ball of twine and let her go higher!"

Marcella did not like to leave Raggedy Ann with the boys, so she sat down on the ground to wait until they pulled down the kite.

But while Marcella watched Raggedy Ann, a dot in the sky, she could not see the wind ripping the rag to which Raggedy was tied.

Suddenly the rag parted and Raggedy Ann went sailing away as the wind caught in her skirts.

Marcella jumped from the ground, too surprised to say anything. The kite, released from the weight of Raggedy

Ann, began darting and swooping to the ground.

"We'll get her for you!" some of the boys said when they saw Marcella's troubled face, and they started running in the direction Raggedy Ann had fallen. Marcella and the other girls ran with them. They ran, and they ran, and they ran, and at last they found the kite upon the ground with one of the sticks broken, but they could not find Raggedy Ann anywhere.

"She must have fallen almost in your yard," a boy said to Marcella, "for the kite was directly over here when the doll fell!"

Marcella was heartbroken. She went in the house and lay on the bed. Mama went out with the other children and tried to find Raggedy Ann, but Raggedy Ann was nowhere to be seen.

When Daddy came home in the evening he tried to find Raggedy, but met with no success. Marcella had eaten hardly any dinner, nor could she be comforted by Mama or Daddy. The other dolls in the nursery lay forgotten and were not put to bed that night, for Marcella lay and sobbed and tossed about in her bed.

Finally she said a little prayer for Raggedy Ann, and went to sleep. And as she slept Marcella dreamed that the Fairies came and took Raggedy Ann with them to Fairyland for a visit, and then sent Raggedy Ann home to her. She awakened with a cry. Of course Mama came to her bed right away and said that Daddy would offer a reward in the morning for the return of Raggedy.

"It was all my fault, Mama!" Marcella said. "I should not have offered the boys dear old Raggedy Ann to tie on the tail of the kite! But I just know the Fairies will send her back."

Mama took her in her arms and soothed her with cheering words, although she felt indeed that Raggedy Ann was truly lost and would never be found again.

Now, where do you suppose Raggedy Ann was all this time?

When Raggedy Ann dropped from the kite, the wind caught in her skirts and carried her along until she fell in the fork of the large elm tree directly over Marcella's house. When Raggedy Ann fell with a thud, face up in the fork of the tree, two robins who had a nest nearby flew away chattering.

Presently the robins returned and quarreled at Raggedy Ann for lying so close to their nest, but Raggedy Ann only smiled at them and did not move.

When the robins quieted down and quit their quarreling, one of them hopped up closer to Raggedy Ann in order to investigate.

It was Mama Robin. She called to Daddy Robin and told him to come. "See the nice yarn! We could use it to line the nest," she said.

So the robins hopped close to Raggedy Ann and asked if they might have some of her yarn hair to line their nests. Raggedy Ann smiled at them. So the two robins pulled and tugged at Raggedy Ann's yarn hair until they had enough to line their nest nice and soft.

Evening came and the robins sang their good-night songs, and Raggedy Ann watched the stars come out, twinkle all night and disappear in the morning light. In the morning the robins again pulled yarn from Raggedy Ann's head and loosened her so she could peep over the side of the limb, and when the sun came up Raggedy Ann saw she was in the tree in her own yard.

Now, before she could eat any breakfast, Marcella started out to find Raggedy Ann. And it was Marcella herself who found her. And this is how she did it.

Mama Robin had seen Marcella with Raggedy Ann out in the yard many times, so she began calling "Cheery! Cheery!" and Daddy Robin started calling "Cheery! Cheery! Cheer up! Cheer up! Cheerily! Cheerily! Cheery! Cheery!" And Marcella, looking up into the tree above the house to see the robins, discovered Raggedy Ann peeping over the limb at her.

Oh, how her heart beat with happiness. "Here is Raggedy Ann!" she shouted as she ran toward the house.

And Mama and Daddy came out and saw Raggedy smiling at them, and Daddy got the clothes prop and climbed out of the attic window and poked Raggedy Ann out of the tree and she fell right into Marcella's arms, where she was hugged in a tight embrace.

"You'll never go up on a kite again, Raggedy Ann," said Marcella, "for I felt so lost without you. I will never let you leave me again."

So Raggedy Ann went into the house and had breakfast with her little mistress and Mama and Daddy smiled at each other when they peeped through the door into the breakfast room, for Raggedy Ann's smile was wide and very yellow. Marcella, her heart full of happiness, was feeding Raggedy Ann part of her egg.

RAGGEDY ANN RESCUES FIDO

IT WAS almost midnight and the dolls were asleep in their beds; all except Raggedy Ann.

Raggedy just lay there, her shoe-button eyes staring straight up at the ceiling. Every once in a while Raggedy Ann ran her rag hand through her yarn hair. She was thinking.

When she had thought for a long, long time, Raggedy Ann raised herself on her wobbly elbows and said, "I've thought it all out."

At this the other dolls shook each other and sat up saying, "Listen! Raggedy has thought it all out!"

"Tell us what you have been thinking, dear Raggedy," said the tin soldier. "We hope they were pleasant thoughts."

"Not very pleasant thoughts!" said Raggedy, as she brushed a tear from her shoe-button eyes. "You haven't seen Fido all day, have you?"

"Not since early this morning," the French dolly said.

"It has troubled me," said Raggedy, "and if my head was not stuffed with lovely new white cotton, I am sure it would have ached with the worry! When Mistress took me into the living room this afternoon she was crying, and I heard her mama say, 'We will find him! He is sure to come home soon!' and I knew they were talking of Fido! He must be lost!"

The tin soldier jumped out of bed and ran over to Fido's basket, his tin feet clicking on the floor as we went. "He is not here," he said.

"When I was sitting in the window about noontime," said the Indian doll, "I saw Fido and a yellow scraggly dog playing out on the lawn and they ran out through a hole in the fence!"

"That was Priscilla's dog, Peterkins!" said the French doll.

"I know poor Mistress is very sad on account of Fido," said the Dutch doll, "because I was in the dining room at suppertime and I heard her daddy tell her to eat her supper and he would go out and find Fido; but I had forgotten all about it until now."

"That is the trouble with all of us except Raggedy Ann!" cried the little penny doll in a squeaky voice. She has to think for all of us!"

"I think it would be a good plan for us to show our love for Mistress and try to find Fido!" exclaimed Raggedy.

"It is a good plan, Raggedy Ann!" cried all the dolls.

"Then let us waste no more time in talking!" said Raggedy Ann, as she jumped from bed, followed by the rest.

The nursery window was open, so the dolls helped each other up on the sill and then jump to the soft grass below. They fell in all sorts of queer positions, but of course the fall did not hurt them.

At the hole in the fence the Indian doll picked up the trail of the two dogs, and the dolls, stringing out behind, followed him until they came to Peterkins' house. Peterkins was surprised to see the strange little figures in white nighties come stringing up the path to the doghouse.

Peterkins was too large to sleep in the nursery, so he had a nice cozy doghouse under the grape arbor.

"Come in," Peterkins said when he saw and recognized the dolls, so all the dollies went into Peterkins' house and sat about while Raggedy told him why they had come.

"It has worried me, too," said Peterkins, "but I had no way of telling your mistress where Fido was, for she cannot understand dog language! For you see," Peterkins continued, "Fido and I were having the grandest romp over in the park when a great big man with a funny thing on the end of a stick came running toward us. We barked at him and Fido thought he was trying to play with us and went up too close and, do you know, that wicked man caught Fido in the thing at the end of the stick and carried him to a wagon and dumped him in with a lot of other dogs!"

"The Dog Catcher!" cried Raggedy Ann.

"Yes!" said Peterkins, as he wiped his eyes with his paws. "It was the dog catcher! For I followed the wagon at a distance and I saw him put all the dogs into a big wire pen, so that none could get out!"

"Then you know the way there, Peterkins?" asked Raggedy Ann.

"Yes, I can find it easily," Peterkins said.

"Then show us the way," Raggedy Ann cried, "for we must try to rescue Fido!"

So Peterkins led the way up alleys and across streets, the dolls all pattering along behind him. It was a strange procession. Once a strange dog ran out at them, but Peterkins told him to mind his own business and the strange dog returned to his own yard.

At last they came to the dog catcher's place. Some of the dogs in the pen were barking at the moon and others were whining and crying.

There was Fido, all covered with mud, and his pretty red ribbon dragging on the ground. My, but he was glad to see the dolls and Peterkins! All the dogs came to the side of the pen and twisted their heads from side to side, gazing in wonder at the queer figures of the dolls.

"We will try and let you out," said Raggedy Ann.

At this all the dogs barked joyfully.

Then Raggedy Ann, the other dolls and Peterkins went to the gate.

The catch was too high for Raggedy Ann to reach, but Peterkins held Raggedy Ann in his mouth and stood up on his hind legs so that she could raise the catch.

When the catch was raised, the dogs were so anxious to get out they pushed and jumped against the gate so hard it flew open, knocking Peterkins and Raggedy Ann into the mud. Such a yapping and barking was never heard in the neighborhood as when the dogs swarmed out of the enclosure, jumping over one another and scrambling about in the mad rush out the gate.

Fido picked himself up from where he had been rolled by the large dogs and helped Raggedy Ann to her feet. He, Peterkins and all the dolls ran after the pack of dogs, turning the corner just as the dog catcher came running out of the house in his nightshirt to see what was causing the trouble.

He stopped in astonishment when he saw the string of dolls in white nighties pattering down the alley, for he could not imagine what they were.

Well, you may be sure the dolls thanked Peterkins for his kind assistance and they and Fido ran on home, for a faint light was beginning to show in the east where the sun was getting ready to come up.

When they got to their own home they found an old chair out in the yard and after a great deal of work they finally dragged it to the window and thus managed to get into the nursery again.

Fido was very grateful to Raggedy Ann and the other dolls and, before he went to his basket, he gave them each a lick on the cheek.

The dolls lost no time in scrambling into bed and pulling up the covers, for they were very sleepy, but just as they

were dozing off, Raggedy Ann raised herself and said, "If my legs and arms were not stuffed with nice clean cotton I feel sure they would ache, but being stuffed with nice clean white cotton, they do not ache and I could not feel happier if my body was stuffed with sunshine, for I know how pleased and happy Mistress will be in the morning when she discovers Fido asleep in his own little basket, safe and sound at home."

And as the dollies by this time were all asleep, Raggedy Ann pulled the sheet up to her chin and smiled so hard she ripped two stitches out of the back of her rag head.

RAGGEDY ANN AND THE STRANGE DOLLS

RAGGEDY ANN lay just as Marcella had dropped her—all sprawled out with her rag arms and legs twisted in ungraceful positions.

Her yarn hair was twisted and lay partly over her face, hiding one of her shoe-button eyes.

Raggedy gave no sign that she had heard, but lay there smiling at the ceiling.

Perhaps Raggedy Ann knew that what the new dolls said was true.

But sometimes the truth may hurt and this may have been the reason Raggedy Ann lay there so still.

"Did you ever see such an ungainly creature!"

"I do believe it has shoe buttons for eyes!"

"And yarn hair!"

"Mercy, did you ever see such feet!"

The Dutch doll rolled off the doll sofa and said "Mama" in his quavery voice, he was so surprised at hearing anyone speak so of beloved Raggedy Ann—she of the candy heart, whom all the dolls loved.

Uncle Clem was also very much surprised and offended. He walked up in front of the two new dolls and looked them sternly in the eyes, but he could think of nothing to say, so he pulled at his yarn mustache.

Marcella received the two new dolls in the morning mail; they were presents from an aunt.

Marcella had named the two new dolls Annabel-Lee and Thomas, after her aunt and uncle.

Annabel-Lee and Thomas were beautiful dolls and must have cost heaps and heaps of shiny pennies, for both were handsomely dressed and had *real* hair!

Annabel's hair was of a lovely shade of auburn and Thomas's was golden yellow.

Annabel was dressed in soft, lace-covered silk and upon her head she wore a beautiful hat with long silk ribbons tied in a neat bow-knot beneath her dimpled chin.

Thomas was dressed in an Oliver Twist suit of dark velvet with a lace collar. Both he and Annabel wore lovely black slippers and short stockings.

They were sitting upon two of the little red chairs where Marcella placed them so they could see the other dolls.

When Uncle Clem walked in front of them and pulled his mustache they laughed outright. "Tee-hee-hee!" they snickered. "He has holes in his knees!"

Quite true. Uncle Clem was made of worsted wool and the moths had eaten his knees and part of his kilt. He had a kilt, you see, for Uncle Clem was a Scotch doll.

Uncle Clem shook, but he felt so hurt he could think of nothing to say.

He walked over and sat down beside Raggedy Ann and brushed her yarn hair away from her shoe-button eye.

The tin soldier went over and sat beside them.

"Don't you mind what they say, Raggedy!" he said. "They don't know you as we do!"

"We don't care to know her!" said Annabel-Lee as she primped her dress. "She looks like a scarecrow!"

"And the soldier must have been made with a can opener!" laughed Thomas.

"You should be ashamed of yourselves!" said the

28

French dolly, as she stood before Annabel and Thomas. "You will make all of us sorry that you have joined our family if you continue to poke fun at us and look down upon us. We are all happy here together and share in each others' adventures and happiness."

Now, that night Marcella did not undress the two new dolls, for she had no nighties for them, so she let them sit up in two little red doll chairs so they would not muss their clothes. "I will make nighties for you tomorrow!" she said as she kissed them good night. Then she went over and gave Raggedy Ann a good-night hug. "Take good care of all my children, Raggedy!" she said as she went out.

Annabel and Thomas whispered together, "Perhaps we have been too hasty in our judgment!" said Annabel-Lee. "This Raggedy Ann seems to be a favorite with the mistress and with all the dolls!"

"There must be a reason!" replied Thomas. "I am beginning to feel sorry that we spoke of her looks. One really cannot help one's looks, after all."

Now, Annabel-Lee and Thomas were very tired after their long journey and soon they fell asleep and forgot all about the other dolls.

When they were sound asleep, Raggedy Ann slipped

quietly from her bed and awakened the tin soldier and Uncle Clem and the three tiptoed to the two beautiful new dolls.

They lifted them gently so as not to awaken them and carried them to Raggedy Ann's bed.

Raggedy Ann tucked them in snugly and lay down upon the hard floor.

The tin soldier and Uncle Clem both tried to coax Raggedy Ann into accepting their bed (they slept together), but Raggedy Ann would not hear of it.

"I am stuffed with nice soft cotton and the hard floor does not bother me at all!" said Raggedy.

The next morning Annabel and Thomas awakened to find themselves in Raggedy Ann's bed and as they raised up and looked at each other, each knew how ashamed the other felt, for they knew Raggedy Ann had generously given them her bed.

There Raggedy Ann lay, all sprawled out upon the hard

floor, her rag arms and legs twisted in ungraceful positions.

"How good and honest she looks!" said Annabel. "It must be her shoe-button eyes!"

"How nicely her yarn hair falls in loops over her face!" exclaimed Thomas. "I did not notice how pleasant her face looked last night!"

"The others seem to love her ever and ever so much!" mused Annabel. "It must be because she is so kind."

Both new dolls were silent for a while, thinking deeply.

"How do you feel?" Thomas finally asked.

"Very much ashamed of myself!" answered Annabel. "And you, Thomas?"

"As soon as Raggedy Ann awakens, I shall tell her just how much ashamed I am of myself and if she can, I want her to forgive me!" Thomas said.

"The more I look at her, the better I like her!" said Annabel.

"I am going to kiss her!" said Thomas.

"You'll awaken her if you do!" said Annabel.

But Thomas climbed out of bed and kissed Raggedy Ann on her painted cheek and smoothed her yarn hair from her rag forehead.

And Annabel-Lee climbed out of bed, too, and kissed Raggedy Ann.

Then Thomas and Annabel-Lee gently carried Raggedy Ann and put her in her own bed and tenderly tucked her in, and then took their seats in the two little red chairs.

After a while Annabel said softly to Thomas, "I feel ever and ever so much better and happier!"

"So do I!" Thomas replied. "It's like a whole lot of sunshine coming into a dark room, and I shall always try to keep it there!"

Fido had one fuzzy white ear sticking up over the edge of his basket and he gave his tail a few thumps against his pillow.

Raggedy Ann lay quietly in bed where Thomas and Annabel had tucked her.   And as she smiled at the ceiling, her candy heart (with "I LOVE YOU" written on it) thrilled with contentment, for, as you have probably guessed, Raggedy Ann had not been asleep at all!

RAGGEDY ANN AND THE KITTENS

RAGGEDY ANN had been away all day.

Marcella had come early in the morning and dressed all the dolls and placed them about the nursery.

Some of the dolls had been put in the little red chairs around the little doll table. There was nothing on the table to eat except a turkey, a fried egg and an apple, all made of plaster of Paris and painted in natural colors. The little teapot and other doll dishes were empty, but Marcella had told them to enjoy their dinner while she was away.

The French dolly had been given a seat upon the doll sofa and Uncle Clem had been placed at the piano.

Marcella picked up Raggedy Ann and carried her out of the nursery when she left, telling the dolls to "be real good children while Mama is away!"

When the door closed, the tin soldier winked at the Dutch doll and handed the imitation turkey to the penny dolls. "Have some nice turkey?" he asked.

"No thank you!" the penny dolls said in little penny-doll, squeaky voices. "We have had all we can eat!"

"Shall I play you a tune?" asked Uncle Clem of the French doll.

At this all the dolls laughed, for Uncle Clem could not begin to play any tune. Raggedy Ann was the only doll who had ever taken lessons, and she could play "Peter, Peter, Pumpkin Eater" with one hand.

In fact, Marcella had almost worn out Raggedy Ann's right hand teaching it to her.

"Play something lively!" said the French doll, as she giggled behind her hand, so Uncle Clem began hammering the eight keys on the toy piano with all his might until a noise was heard upon the stairs.

Quick as a wink, all the dolls took the same positions in which they had been placed by Marcella, for they did not really truly wish people to know that they could move about.

But it was only Fido. He put his nose in the door and looked around.

All the dolls at the table looked steadily at the painted food, and Uncle Clem leaned upon the piano keys looking just as unconcerned as when he had been placed there.

Then Fido pushed the door open and came into the nursery wagging his tail.

He walked over to the table and sniffed, in hopes Marcella had given the dolls real food and that some would still be left.

"Where's Raggedy Ann?" Fido asked, when he had satisfied himself that there was no food.

"Mistress took Raggedy Ann and went somewhere!" all the dolls answered in chorus.

"I've found something I must tell Raggedy Ann about!" said Fido, as he scratched his ear.

"Is it a secret?" asked the penny dolls.

"Secret nothing," replied Fido. "It's kittens!"

"How lovely!" cried all the dolls. Real live kittens?"

"Real live kittens!" replied Fido. "Three little tiny ones, out in the barn!"

"Oh, I wish Raggedy Ann was here!" cried the French doll. "She would know what to do about it!"

"That's why I wanted to see her," said Fido, as he

thumped his tail on the floor. "I did not know there were any kittens and I went into the barn to hunt for mice and the first thing I knew Mama Cat came right at me with her eyes looking green! I tell you, I hurried out of there!"

"How did you know there were any kittens, then?" asked Uncle Clem.

"I waited around the barn until Mama Cat went up to the house and then I slipped into the barn again, for I knew there must be something inside or she would not have jumped at me that way! We are always very friendly, you know." Fido continued. "And what was my surprise to find three tiny little kittens in an old basket, way back in a dark corner!"

"Go get them, Fido, and bring them up so we can see them!" said the tin soldier.

"Not me!" said Fido. "If I had a suit of tin clothes on like you have I might do it, but you know cats can scratch very hard if they want to!"

"We will tell Raggedy when she comes in!" said the French doll, and Fido went out to play with a neighbor dog.

So when Raggedy Ann had been returned to the nursery the dolls could hardly wait until Marcella had put on their nighties and left them for the night.

Then they told Raggedy Ann all about the kittens.

Raggedy Ann jumped from her bed and ran over to Fido's basket; he wasn't there.

Then Raggedy suggested that all the dolls go out to the barn and see the kittens. This they did easily, for the window was open and it was but a short jump to the ground.

They found Fido out near the barn watching a hole.

"I was afraid something might disturb them," he said, "for Mama Cat went away about an hour ago."

All the dolls, with Raggedy Ann in the lead, crawled through the hole and ran to the basket.

Just as Raggedy Ann started to pick up one of the kittens there was a lot of howling and yelping and Fido came bounding through the hole with Mama Cat behind him. When Mama Cat caught up with Fido he would yelp.

When Fido and Mama Cat had circled the barn two or

three times Fido managed to find the hole and escape to the yard; then Mama Cat came over to the basket and saw all the dolls.

"I'm surprised at you, Mama Cat!" said Raggedy Ann. "Fido has been watching your kittens for an hour while you were away. He wouldn't hurt them for anything!"

"I'm sorry, then," said Mama Cat.

"You must trust Fido, Mama Cat," said Raggedy Ann, "because he loves you and anyone who loves you can be trusted!"

"That's so!" replied Mama Cat. "Cats love mice, too, and I wish the mice trusted us more!"

The dolls all laughed at this joke.

"Have you told the folks up at the house about your dear little kittens?" Raggedy Ann asked.

"Oh, my, no!" exclaimed Mama Cat. "At the last place I lived the people found out about my kittens and do you know, all the kittens disappeared! I intend keeping this a secret!"

"But all the folks at this house are very kind people and would dearly love your kittens!" cried all the dolls.

"Let's take them right up to the nursery!" said Raggedy Ann. "And Mistress can find them there in the morning!"

"How lovely!" said all the dolls in chorus. "Do, Mama Cat! Raggedy Ann knows, for she is stuffed with nice clean white cotton and is very wise!"

So after a great deal of persuasion, Mama Cat finally consented. Raggedy Ann took two of the kittens and carried them to the house while Mama Cat carried the other.

Raggedy Ann wanted to give the kittens her bed, but Fido, who was anxious to prove his affection, insisted that Mama Cat and the kittens should have his nice soft basket.

The dolls could hardly sleep that night; they were so anxious to see what Mistress would say when she found the

dear little kittens there in Fido's basket next morning.

Raggedy Ann did not sleep a wink, for she shared her bed with Fido and he kept her awake whispering to her.

In the morning when Marcella came to the nursery, the first thing she saw were the three little kittens.

She cried out in delight and carried them all down to show to Mama and Daddy. Mama Cat was trailing along, arching her back and purring with pride as she rubbed against all the chairs and doors.

Mama and Daddy said the kittens could stay in the nursery and belong to Marcella, so Marcella took them back to Fido's basket while she hunted names for them out of a fairy-tale book.

Marcella finally decided upon three names: Prince Charming for the white kitty, Cinderella for the Maltese and Princess Golden for the kitty with the yellow stripes.

So that is how the three little kittens came to live in the nursery.

And it all turned out just as Raggedy Ann had said, for her head was stuffed with clean white cotton, and she could think exceedingly wise thoughts.

And Mama Cat found out that Fido was a very good friend, too. She grew to trust him so much she would even let him help wash the kittens' faces.

RAGGEDY ANN AND THE CHICKENS

WHEN Marcella was called into the house she left Raggedy sitting on the chicken yard fence. "Now you sit quietly and do not stir," Marcella told Raggedy Ann. "If you move you may fall and hurt yourself!"

So, Raggedy Ann sat quietly, just as Marcella told her, but she smiled at the chickens, for she had fallen time and again and it had never hurt her in the least. She was stuffed with nice soft cotton, you see.

So, there she sat until a tiny little hummingbird, in search of flower honey, hummed close to Raggedy Ann's head and hovered near the tall hollyhocks.

Raggedy Ann turned to see the hummingbird and lost her balance—*plump!* she went, down among the chickens.

The chickens scattered in all directions, all except Old Ironsides, the rooster.

He ruffled his neck feathers and put his head down close to the ground, making a queer whistling noise as he looked fiercely at Raggedy Ann.

But Raggedy Ann only smiled at Old Ironsides, the rooster, and ran her rag hand through her yarn hair, for she did not fear him.

Then something strange happened; when she made this motion the old rooster jumped in the air and kicked his feet out in front, knocking Raggedy Ann over and over.

When Raggedy Ann stopped rolling she waved her apron at the rooster and cried, "Shoo!" but instead of "shooing," Old Ironsides upset her again.

Now two old hens who had been watching the rooster jump at Raggedy ran up and, as one old hen placed herself in front of the rooster, the old hen caught hold of Raggedy's apron and dragged her into the chicken coop.

It was dark inside and Raggedy could not tell what was going on as she felt herself being pulled up over the nests.

But finally Raggedy could sit up, for the old hen had quit pulling her, and as her shoe-button eyes were very good, she soon made out the shape of the old hen in front of her.

"My! That's the hardest work I have done in a long time!" said the old hen, when she could catch her breath. "I was afraid Mr. Rooster would tear your dress!"

"That was a queer game he was playing, Mrs. Hen," said Raggedy Ann.

The old hen chuckled way down in her throat, "Gracious me! He wasn't playing a game, he was fighting you!"

"Fighting!" cried Raggedy Ann in surprise.

"Oh yes, indeed!" the old hen answered. "Old Ironsides, the rooster, thought you intended to harm some of the baby chickens and he was fighting you!"

"I am sorry that I fell inside the pen. I wouldn't harm anything," Raggedy Ann said.

"If we tell you a secret you must promise not to tell your mistress!" said the old hens.

"I promise! Cross my candy heart!" said Raggedy Ann.

Then the two old hens took Raggedy Ann way back in the farthest corner of the chicken coop. There, in back of

a box, they had built two nests and each old hen had ten eggs in her nest.

"If your folks hear of it they will take the eggs," said the hens, "and then we could not raise our families!"

Raggedy Ann felt the eggs and they were nice and warm.

"We just left the nests when you fell into the pen!" explained the old hens.

"But how can the eggs grow if you sit upon them?" said Raggedy. "If Fido sits on any of the garden, the plants will not grow, Mistress says!"

"Eggs are different!" one old hen explained. "In order to make the eggs hatch properly, we must sit on them three weeks and not let them get cold at any time!"

"And at the end of the three weeks do the eggs sprout?" asked Raggedy Ann.

"You must be thinking of eggplant!" cried one old hen. "These eggs hatch at the end of three weeks—they don't sprout—and then we have a lovely family of soft downy chickies to cuddle under our wings and love dearly!"

"Have you been sitting upon the eggs very long?" Raggedy asked.

"Neither one of us has kept track of the time," said one

hen. "You see, we never leave the nests, only just once in a while to get a drink and to eat a little. So we can hardly tell when it is day and when it is night."

"We were going out to get a drink when you fell in the pen!" said one old hen. "Now we will have to sit upon the eggs and warm them up again!"

The two old hens spread their feathers and nestled down upon the nests.

"When you get them good and warm, I would be glad to sit upon the eggs and keep them warm until you get something to eat and drink!" said Raggedy. So the two old hens walked out of the coop to finish their meal, which had been interrupted by Raggedy's fall, and while they were gone Raggedy Ann sat quietly upon the warm eggs. Suddenly down beneath her she heard something go, *"Pick, pick!"* "I hope it isn't a mouse!" Raggedy Ann said to herself when she felt something move. "I wish the old hens would come back." But when they came back and saw the puzzled expression on her face, they cried, "What is it?"

Raggedy Ann got to her feet and looked down and there were several little fluffy, cuddly baby chickies, round as little puff balls.

"Cheep! Cheep! Cheep!" they cried.

"Baby chicks!" Raggedy cried, as she stooped and picked up one of the little puff balls.

The two old hens, their eyes shining with happiness, got upon the nests and spread out their soft warm feathers. "The others eggs will hatch soon!" they said.

So, for several days Raggedy helped the two hens hatch out the rest of the chickies and just as they finished, Marcella came inside looking around.

"How in the world did you get in here, Raggedy Ann?" she cried. "I have been looking all over for you! Did the chickens drag you in here?"

Both old hens down behind the box clucked softly to the chickies beneath them and Marcella overheard them.

She lifted the box away and gave a little squeal of surprise and happiness.

"Oh, you dear old Hennypennies!" she cried, lifting both old hens from their nests. "You have hidden your nests away back here and now you have one, two, three, four—twenty chickies!" and as she counted them, Marcella placed them in her apron; then picking up Raggedy Ann, she placed her over the new little chickies.

"Come on, old Hennypennies!" she said, and went out of the coop with the two old hens clucking at her heels.

Marcella called Daddy and Daddy rolled two barrels out under one of the trees and made a nice bed in each. Then he nailed slats across the front, leaving a place for a door. Each Hennypenny was then given ten little chickies and shut up in the barrel. And all the dolls were happy when they heard of Raggedy's adventure and they soon were all taken out to see the new chickies.

RAGGEDY ANN'S NEW SISTERS

MARCELLA was having a tea party up in the nursery when Daddy called to her, so she left the dollies sitting around the tiny table and ran downstairs carrying Raggedy Ann with her.

Mama, Daddy and a strange man were talking in the living room and Daddy introduced Marcella to the stranger.

The stranger was a large man with kindly eyes and a cheery smile, as pleasant as Raggedy Ann's.

He took Marcella upon his knee and ran his fingers through her curls as he talked to Daddy and Mama, so, of course, Raggedy Ann liked him from the beginning. "I have two little girls," he told Marcella. "Their names are Virginia and Doris, and one time when we were at the seashore they were playing in the sand and they covered up Freddy, Doris' boy-doll in the sand. They were pretending that Freddy was bathing and that he wanted to be covered with the clean white sand, just as the other bathers did. And when they had covered Freddy they took their little pails and shovels and went farther down the beach to play and forgot all about Freddy.

"Now, when it came time for us to go home, Virginia and Doris remembered Freddy and ran down to get him, but the tide had come in and Freddy was way out under the water and they could not find him. Virginia and Doris were very sad and they talked of Freddy all the way home.''

"It was too bad they forgot Freddy," said Marcella.

"Yes, indeed it was!" the new friend replied as he took Raggedy Ann up and made her dance on Marcella's knee. "But it turned out all right after all, for do you know what happened to Freddy?"

"No, what did happen to him?" Marcella asked.

"Well, first of all, when Freddy was covered with the sand, he enjoyed it immensely. And he did not mind it so much when the tide came up over him, for he felt Virginia and Doris would return and get him.

"But presently Freddy felt the sand above him move as if someone was digging him out. Soon his head was uncovered and he could look right up through the pretty green water, and what do you think was happening? The Tide Fairies were uncovering Freddy!

"When he was completely uncovered, the Tide Fairies swam with Freddy way out to the Undertow Fairies. The Undertow Fairies took Freddy and swam with him way out to the Roller Fairies. The Roller Fairies carried Freddy up to the surface and tossed him up to the Spray Fairies, who carried him to the Wind Fairies.''

"And the Wind Fairies?" Marcella asked breathlessly.

"The Wind Fairies carried Freddy right to our garden and there Virginia and Doris found him, none the worse for his wonderful adventure!''

"Freddy must have enjoyed it and your little girls must have been very glad to get Freddy back again!" said Marcella. "Raggedy Ann went up in the air on the tail of a kite one day and fell, so now I am very careful with her!''

"Would you let me take Raggedy Ann for a few days?" asked the new friend.

Marcella was silent. She liked the stranger friend, but she did not wish to lose Raggedy Ann.

"I will promise to take good care of her and return her in a week. Will you let her go with me, Marcella?"

Marcella finally agreed and when the stranger friend left, he placed Raggedy Ann in his bag.

"It is lonely without Raggedy Ann!" said the dollies each night.

"We miss her happy painted smile and her cheery ways!" they said.

And so the week dragged by. . . .

But, my! What a chatter there was in the nursery the first night after Raggedy Ann returned. All the dolls were so anxious to hug Raggedy Ann they could scarcely wait until Marcella had left them alone.

When they had squeezed Raggedy Ann almost out of shape and she had smoothed out her hair, patted her apron out and felt her shoe-button eyes to see if they were still there, she said, "Well, what have you been doing? Tell me all the news!"

"Oh, we have just had the usual tea parties and games!" said the tin soldier. "Tell us about yourself, Raggedy dear, we have missed you so much!"

"Yes! Tell us where you have been and what you have done, Raggedy!" all the dolls cried.

But Raggedy Ann just then noticed that one of the penny dolls had a hand missing.

"How did this happen?" she asked as she picked up the doll.

"I fell off the table and landed upon the tin soldier last night when we were playing. But don't mind a little thing like that, Raggedy Ann," replied the penny doll. "Tell us of yourself! Have you had a nice time?"

"I shall not tell a thing until your hand is mended!" Raggedy Ann said.

So the Indian doll ran and brought a bottle of glue.
"Where's the hand?" Raggedy asked.

"In my pocket," the penny doll answered.

When Raggedy Ann had glued the penny doll's hand in
place and wrapped a rag around it to hold it until the glue
dried, she said, "When I tell you of this wonderful adventure, I know you will all feel very happy. It has made me
almost burst my stitches with joy."

The dolls all sat upon the floor around Raggedy Ann,
the tin soldier with his arm over her shoulder.

"Well, first when I left," said Raggedy Ann, "I was
placed in the stranger friend's bag. It was rather stuffy
in there, but I did not mind it; in fact I believe I must
have fallen asleep, for when I awakened I saw the stranger
friend's hand reaching into the bag. Then he lifted me
from the bag and danced me upon his knee. 'What do you
think of her?' he said to three other men sitting nearby.

"I was so interested in looking out of the window I did

53

not pay any attention to what they said, for we were on a train and the scenery was just flying by! Then I was put back in the bag.

"When next I was taken from the bag, I was in a large, clean, light room and there were many, many girls all dressed in white aprons.

"The stranger friend showed me to another man and to the girls, who took off my clothes, cut my seams and took out my cotton. And what do you think! They found my lovely candy heart had not melted at all as I had thought. Then they laid me on a table and marked all around my outside edges with a pencil on clean white cloth, and then the girls re-stuffed me and dressed me.

"I stayed in a clean, big, light room for two or three days and nights and watched my sisters grow from pieces of cloth into rag dolls just like myself!"

"Your SISTERS!" the dolls all exclaimed in astonishment. "What do you mean, Raggedy?"

"I mean," said Raggedy Ann, "that the stranger friend had borrowed me from Marcella so that he could have patterns made from me. And before I left the big, clean, white room there were hundreds of rag dolls so like me you would not have been able to tell us apart."

"We could have told *you* by your happy smile!" cried the French dolly.

"But all of my sister dolls have smiles just like mine!" replied Raggedy Ann.

"And shoe-button eyes?" the dolls all asked.

"Yes, shoe-button eyes!" Raggedy Ann replied.

"I could tell you from the others by your dress, Raggedy Ann," said the French doll. Your dress is seventy years old! I could tell you by that!"

"But my new sister rag dolls have dresses just like mine, for the stranger friend had cloth made especially for them exactly like mine."

"I know how we could tell you from the other rag dolls, even if you all look exactly alike!" said the Indian doll, who had been thinking for a long time as he sat quietly in his corner.

"How?" asked Raggedy Ann with a laugh.

"By feeling your candy heart! If the doll has a candy heart, then it is you, Raggedy Ann!"

Raggedy Ann laughed, "I am so glad you all love me as you do, but I am sure you would not be able to tell me from my new sisters, except that I am more worn, for each new rag doll has a candy heart, and on it is written 'I LOVE YOU,' just as is written on my own candy heart."

"And there are hundreds and hundreds of the new rag dolls?" asked the little penny dolls.

"Hundreds and hundreds of them, all named Raggedy Ann," replied Raggedy.

"Then," said the penny dolls, "we are indeed happy and proud for you! For wherever one of the new Raggedy Ann dolls goes, there will go with it the love and happiness that *you* give to others."

The Original Adventures of
Raggedy Andy

To
Marcella's Mama

Gainesville, Florida

Johnny Gruelle
South Norwalk
Connecticut

Dear Johnny :

WHEN I saw your *Raggedy Ann* books and dolls in a store near here, I went right in and bought one of each, and when I had read your introduction to *Raggedy Ann* I went right up to an old trunk in my own attic and brought down the doll I am sending you with this letter.

This doll belonged to my mother and she played with it when a little girl. She treasured it highly, I know, for she kept it until I came and then she gave it to me.

The fun that we two have had together I cannot begin to tell you, but often, like the little boy who went out into the garden to eat worms when all the world seemed blue and clouded, this doll and I went out under the arbor and had our little cry together. I can still feel its soft rag arms (as I used to imagine) about me, and hear the words of comfort (also imaginary) that were whispered in my ear.

As you say in your *Raggedy Ann* book, ''Fairyland must be filled with rag dolls, soft loppy rag dolls who go through all the beautiful adventures found there, nestling in the crook of a dimpled arm.'' I truly believe there is such a Fairyland and that rag dolls were first made there, or how else could they bring so much sunshine into a child's life?

All the little girls of my acquaintance have your *Raggedy Ann* book and doll, and for the happiness you have brought to them, let me give to you the doll of all my dolls, the doll I love most dearly.

May it prove to you a gift from Fairyland, bringing with it all the "wish come true" that you may wish and, if possible, add to the sunshine in your life.

My mother called the doll Raggedy Andy and it was by this name that I have always known him. Is it any wonder that I was surprised when I saw the title of your book?

Introduce Raggedy Andy to Raggedy Ann, dear Johnny. Let him share in the happiness of your household.

Sincerely yours,

Raggedy Andy's "Mama"

Wilton, Connecticut

Dear John:

YOUR LETTER brings many pleasant memories to my
mind and takes me back to my childhood.

Living next door to us, when I was about four years old,
was a little girl named Bessie. I cannot recall her last
name. When my mother made Raggedy Ann for me, Bessie's mother made a rag doll for her, for we two always
played together. As I recall, there was no fence between
our two houses.

Bessie's doll was made a day or so after Raggedy Ann,
I think, though I am not quite certain which of the dolls
was made first. However, Bessie's doll was given the name
of Raggedy Andy, and one of the two dolls was named
after the other, so that their names would sound alike.

We children played with the two rag dolls most of the
time until Bessie's family moved away—when I was eight
or nine years old. They had faces just alike. The mother
who made the first doll probably painted both doll faces.
I do not remember just how Raggedy Andy was dressed,
but I know he often wore dresses over his boy clothes when
Bessie and I decided that he and Raggedy Ann should be
sisters for the day.

You remember I told you about Raggedy Andy long
ago. Isn't it strange that the two old rag dolls should come
together after all these years? I wish Raggedy Andy's
''Mama'' had signed her name, for I should like to write
to her. Perhaps there may be some way of finding her out.

Anyway, it seems to me you have the subject for another
rag doll book, for Raggedy Andy must have had some
wonderful adventures in his long life.

Yours lovingly,

Mom

HOW RAGGEDY ANDY CAME

ONE DAY Daddy took Raggedy Ann down to his office and propped her up against some books upon his desk. He wanted to have her where he could see her cheery smile all day, for, as you must surely know, smiles and happiness are truly catching.

Daddy wished to catch a whole lot of Raggedy Ann's cheeriness and happiness and put all this down on paper, so that those who did not have Raggedy Ann dolls might see just how happy and smiling a rag doll can be.

So Raggedy Ann stayed at Daddy's studio for three or four days.

She was missed very, very much at home and Marcella really longed for her, but knew that Daddy was borrowing some of Raggedy Ann's sunshine, so she did not complain.

Raggedy Ann did not complain either, for in addition to the sunny, happy smile she always wore (it was painted on), Raggedy Ann had a candy heart, and of course no one (not even a rag doll) ever complains if they have such happiness about them.

One evening, just as Daddy was finishing his day's work, a messenger boy came with a package—a nice, soft lumpy package.

Daddy opened the nice, soft lumpy package and found a letter.

Grandma had told Daddy, long before this, that at the time Raggedy Ann was made, a neighbor lady had made a boy-doll, Raggedy Andy, for her little girl, who always played with Grandma.

And when Grandma told Daddy this she wondered whatever had become of her little playmate and the boy-doll, Raggedy Andy.

After reading the letter, Daddy opened the other package which had been inside the nice, soft, lumpy package and found —Raggedy Andy!

Raggedy Andy had been carefully folded up. His soft, loppy arms were folded up in front of him and his soft, loppy legs were folded over his soft, loppy arms, and they were held this way by a rubber band.

Raggedy Andy must have wondered why he was being arranged this way, but it could not have caused him any worry, for in between where his feet came over his face Daddy saw his cheery smile.

After slipping off the rubber band, Daddy smoothed out the wrinkles in Raggedy Andy's arms and legs.

Then Daddy propped Raggedy Ann and Raggedy Andy up against books on his desk, so that they sat facing each other. Raggedy Ann's shoe-button eyes looking straight into the shoe-button eyes of Raggedy Andy.

They could not speak—not right out before a real person—so they just sat there and smiled at each other.

Daddy could not help reaching out his hands and feeling their throats.

Yes! There was a lump in Raggedy Ann's throat, and there was a lump in Raggedy Andy's throat. A cotton lump, to be sure, but a lump nevertheless.

"So, Raggedy Ann and Raggedy Andy, that is why you cannot talk, is it?" said Daddy.

"I will go away and let you have your visit to yourselves, although it is good to sit and share your happiness by watching you."

Daddy then took the rubber band and placed it around Raggedy Ann's right hand and around Raggedy Andy's right hand, so that when he had it fixed properly they sat and held each other's hands.

Daddy knew they would wish to tell each other all the wonderful things that had happened to them since they had parted more than sixty years before.

So, locking his studio door, Daddy left the two old rag dolls looking into each other's eyes.

Then next morning, when Daddy unlocked his door and looked at his desk, he saw that Raggedy Andy had fallen over so that he lay with his head in the bend of Raggedy Ann's arm.

THE NURSERY DANCE

WHEN Raggedy Andy was first brought to the nursery he was very quiet.

Raggedy Andy did not speak all day, but he smiled pleasantly to all the other dolls. There was Raggedy Ann, the French doll, the little Dutch doll, the tin soldier, Uncle Clem and a few others.

Some of the dolls were without arms and legs.

One had a cracked head. She was a nice doll, though, and the others all liked her very much.

All of them had cried the night Susan (that was her name) fell off the toy box and cracked her china head.

Raggedy Andy did not speak all day.

But there was really nothing strange about this fact, after all.

None of the other dolls spoke all day, either.

Marcella had played in the nursery all day and of course they did not speak in front of her.

Marcella thought they did, though, and often had them saying things which they really were not even thinking of.

For instance, when Marcella served water with sugar in it and little oyster crackers for "tea," Raggedy Andy was thinking of Raggedy Ann, and the French doll was thinking of one time when Fido was lost.

Marcella took the French doll's hand and passed a cup of tea to Raggedy Andy, and said, "Mr. Raggedy Andy, will you have another cup of tea?" as if the French doll was talking.

And then Marcella answered for Raggedy Andy, "Oh, yes, thank you! It is so delicious!"

Neither the French doll nor Raggedy Andy knew what was going on, for they were thinking real hard to themselves.

Nor did they drink the tea when it was poured for them. Marcella drank it instead.

Perhaps this was just as well, for most of the dolls were moist inside from the tea of the day before.

Marcella did not always drink all of the tea. Often she poured a little down their mouths.

Sugar and water, if taken in small quantities, would not give the dolls colic, Marcella would tell them, but she did not know that it made their cotton or sawdust insides quite sticky.

Quite often, too, Marcella forgot to wash their faces after a "tea," and Fido would do it for them when he came into the nursery and found the dolls with sweets upon their faces.

Really, Fido was quite a help in this way, but he often missed the corners of their eyes and the backs of their necks, where the tea would run and get sticky. But he did his best and saved his little mistress a lot of work.

No, Raggedy Andy did not speak. He merely thought a great deal.

One can, you know, when one has been a rag doll as long as Raggedy Andy had. Years and years and years and years!

Even Raggedy Ann, with all her wisdom, did not really know how long Raggedy Andy and she had been rag dolls.

If Raggedy Ann had a pencil in her rag hand and Marcella guided it for her, Raggedy Ann could count up to ten —sometimes. But why should one worry one's rag head about one's age when all one's life has been one happy experience after another, with each day filled with love and sunshine?

Raggedy Andy did not know his age, but he remembered many things that had happened years and years and years ago, when he and Raggedy Ann were quite young.

It was of these pleasant times Raggedy Andy was thinking all day, and this was the reason he did not notice that Marcella was speaking for him.

Raggedy Andy could patiently wait until Marcella put all the dollies to bed and left them for the night, alone in the nursery.

The day might have passed very slowly had it not been for the happy memories that filled Raggedy Andy's cotton-stuffed head.

But he did not even fidget.

Of course, he fell out of his chair once, and his shoe-button eyes went *"Click!"* against the floor, but it wasn't his fault. Raggedy Andy was so loppy he could hardly be placed in a chair so that he would stay, and Marcella jiggled the table.

Marcella cried for Raggedy Andy, *"AWAA! AWAA!"* and picked him up and snuggled him and scolded Uncle Clem for jiggling the table.

Through all this Raggedy Andy kept right on thinking his pleasant thoughts, and really did not know he had fallen from the chair.

So you see how easy it is to pass over the little bumps of life if we are happy inside.

And Raggedy Andy was quiet all day, and the day finally passed.

Raggedy Andy was given one of Uncle Clem's clean white nighties and shared Uncle Clem's bed. Marcella kissed them all good night and left them to sleep until morning.

But as soon as she left the room all the dolls sat up in their beds. When their little mistress' footsteps passed out of hearing, all the dollies jumped out of their beds and gathered around Raggedy Andy.

Raggedy Ann introduced them one by one and Raggedy Andy shook hands with each.

''I am very happy to know you all,'' he said in a voice

as kindly as Raggedy Ann's, "and I hope we will all like each other as much as Raggedy Ann and I have always liked each other!"

"Oh, indeed we shall!" the dollies all answered. "We love Raggedy Ann because she is so kindly and happy, and we know we shall like you, too, for you talk like Raggedy Ann and have the same cheery smile!"

"Now that we know each other so well, what do you say to a game, Uncle Clem?" Raggedy Andy cried, as he caught Uncle Clem and danced about the floor.

The Dutch doll dragged the little square music box out into the center of the room and wound it up. Then all,

holding hands, danced in a circle around it, laughing and shouting in their tiny doll voices.

"That was lots of fun!" Raggedy Andy said, when the music stopped and all the dolls had taken seats upon the floor facing him. "You know, I have been shut in a trunk up in an attic for years and years and years."

"Wasn't it very lonesome in the trunk all that time?" Susan asked in her queer little cracked voice.

"Oh, not at all," Raggedy Andy replied, "for there was always a nest of mice down in the corner of the trunk. Cute little Mama and Daddy mice, and lots of little teeny-weeny baby mice. And when Mama and Daddy mice were away, I used to cuddle the tiny little baby mice!"

"No wonder you were never lonesome!" said Uncle Clem, who was very kind and loved everybody and everything.

"No, I was never lonesome in the old trunk in the attic, but it is far more pleasant to be out again and living here with all you nice friends!" said Raggedy Andy.

And all the dolls thought so, too, for already they loved Raggedy Andy's happy smile and knew he would prove to be as kindly and lovable as Raggedy Ann.

THE RABBIT CHASE

"WELL, what shall we play tonight?" asked the Dutch doll when the house was quiet and the dolls all knew that no one else was awake.

Raggedy Andy was just about to suggest a good game, when Fido, who sometimes slept in a basket in the nursery, growled.

All the dollies looked in his direction.

Fido was standing up with his ears sticking as straight in the air as loppy puppy-dog ears can stick up.

"He must have been dreaming!" said Raggedy Andy.

"No, I wasn't dreaming!" Fido answered. "I heard something go, *'Scratch! Scratch!'* as plain as I hear you!"

"Where did the sound come from, Fido?" Raggedy Andy asked when he saw that Fido really was wide awake.

"From outside somewhere!" Fido answered. "And if I could get out without disturbing all the folks, I'd run out and see what it might be! Perhaps I had better bark!"

"Please do not bark!" Raggedy Andy cried as he put his rag arm around Fido's nose. "You will wake up everybody in the house. We can open a door or a window for you and let you out, if you must go!"

"I wish you would. Listen! There it is again— *'Scratch! Scratch!'* What can it be?"

"You may soon see!" said Raggedy Andy. "We'll let you out, but please don't sit at the door and bark and bark to get back in again, as you usually do, for we are going to play a good game and we may not hear you!"

"You can sleep out in the shed after you have found out what it is," said Raggedy Andy.

As soon as the dolls opened the door for Fido, he went running across the lawn, barking in a loud shrill voice. He

ran down behind the shed and through the garden, and then back toward the house again.

Raggedy Andy and Uncle Clem stood looking out of the door, the rest of the dolls peeping over their shoulders, so when something came jumping through the door, it hit Uncle Clem and Raggedy Andy and sent them flying against the other dolls behind them.

All the dolls went down in a wiggling heap on the floor.

It was surprising that the noise and confusion did not wake Daddy and the rest of the folks, for just as the dolls were untangling themselves from each other and getting up on their feet, Fido came jumping through the door and sent the dolls tumbling again.

Fido quit barking when he came through the door.

"Which way did he go?" he asked, when he could get his breath.

"What was it?" Raggedy Andy asked in return.

"It was a rabbit!" Fido cried. "He ran right in here, for I could smell his tracks!"

"We could feel him!" Raggedy Andy laughed.

"I could not tell you which way he went," Uncle Clem said, "except I feel sure he came through the door and into the house!"

None of the dolls knew into which room the rabbit had run.

Finally, after much sniffing, Fido traced the rabbit to the nursery, where, when the dolls followed, they saw the rabbit crouching behind the rocking horse.

Fido whined and cried because he could not get to the rabbit and bite him.

"You should be ashamed of yourself, Fido!" cried Raggedy Ann. "Just see how the poor bunny is trembling!"

"He should not come scratching around our house if he doesn't care to be chased!" said Fido.

"Why don't you stay out in the woods and fields where you really belong?" Raggedy Andy asked the rabbit.

"I came to leave some Easter eggs!" the bunny answered in a queer little quavery voice.

"An Easter bunny!" all the dolls cried, jumping about and clapping their hands. "An Easter bunny!"

"Well!" was all Fido could say, as he sat down and began wagging his tail.

"You may come out from behind the rocking horse now, Easter bunny!" said Raggedy Andy. "Fido will not hurt you now that he knows, will you, Fido?"

"Indeed I won't!" Fido replied. "I'm sorry that I chased you! And I remember now, I had to jump over a basket out by the shed! Was that yours?"

"Yes, it was full of Easter eggs and colored grasses for the little girl who lives here!" the bunny said.

When the Easter bunny found out that Fido and the dolls were his friends, he came out from behind the rocking horse and hopped across the floor to the door.

"I must go see if any of the eggs are broken, for if they are, I will have to run home and color some more! I was just about to make a nice nest and put the eggs in it when Fido came bouncing out at me!"

And with a squeaky little laugh the Easter bunny, followed by Fido and all the dolls, hopped across the lawn toward the shed. There they found the basket. Four of the lovely colored Easter eggs were broken.

"I will run home and color four more. It will only take a few minutes, so when I return and scratch again to make a nest, please do not bark at me!" said the Easter bunny.

"I won't! I promise!" Fido laughed.

"May we go with you and watch you color the Easter eggs?" Raggedy Andy begged.

"Indeed you may!" the Easter bunny answered. "Can you run fast?"

Then down through the garden and out through a crack in the fence the Easter bunny hopped, with a long string of dolls trailing behind.

When they came to the Easter bunny's home, they found Mama Easter bunny and a lot of little teeny-weeny bunnies who would someday grow up to be big Easter bunnies like their Mama and Daddy bunnies.

The Easter bunny told them of his adventure with Fido, and all joined in his laughter when they found it had turned out well in the end.

The Easter bunny put four eggs on to boil and while these were boiling he mixed up a lot of pretty colors.

When the eggs were boiled, he dipped them into the pretty colored dyes and then painted lovely flowers on them.

When the Easter bunny had finished painting the eggs he put them in his basket and, with all the dolls running along beside him, they returned to the house.

"Why not make the nest right in the nursery?" Raggedy Andy asked.

"That would be just the thing! Then the little girl would wonder and wonder how I could ever get into the

nursery without waking the rest of the folks, for she will never suspect that you dolls and Fido let me in!''

So with Raggedy Andy leading the way, they ran up to the nursery and there, way back in a corner, they watched the Easter bunny make a lovely nest and put the Easter eggs in it.

And in the morning, when Marcella came in to see the dolls, you can imagine her surprise when she found the pretty gift of the Easter bunny.

''How in the world did the bunny get inside the house and into this room without waking Fido?'' she laughed.

And Fido, pretending to be asleep, slowly opened one eye and winked over the edge of his basket at Raggedy Andy.

And Raggedy Andy smiled back at Fido, but never said a word.

THE NEW TIN GUTTER

ALL DAY Saturday the men had worked up on the roof of the house and the dolls facing the window could see them.

The men made quite a lot of noise with their hammers, for they were putting new gutters around the eaves, and pounding upon tin makes a great deal of noise.

Marcella had not played with the dolls all that day, for she had gone visiting, so when the men hammered and made a lot of noise, the dolls could talk to each other without fear of anyone hearing or knowing they were really talking to each other.

"What are they doing now?" Raggedy Andy asked.

He was lying with his head beneath a little bed quilt, just as Marcella had dropped him when she left the nursery, so he could not see what was going on.

"We can only see the men's legs as they pass the window," answered Uncle Clem. "But they are putting new shingles or something on the roof!"

After the men had left their work and gone home to supper and the house was quiet, Raggedy Andy cautiously moved his head out from under the little bed quilt and, seeing that the coast was clear, sat up.

This was a signal for all the dolls to sit up and smooth out the wrinkles in their clothes.

The nursery window was open, so Raggedy Andy lifted the penny dolls to the sill and climbed up beside them.

Leaning out, he could look along the new shiny tin gutter the men had put in place.

"Here's a grand place to have a lovely slide!" he said as he gave one of the penny dolls a scoot down the shiny tin gutter.

"*Whee!* See her go!" Raggedy Andy cried.

All the other dolls climbed up on the windowsill beside him.

Scoot me, too!" cried the other little penny doll in her squeaky little voice, and Raggedy Andy took her in his rag hand and gave her a great swing that sent her scooting down the shiny tin gutter, *"Kerswish!"*

Then Raggedy Andy climbed into the gutter himself and, taking a few steps, spread out his feet and went scooting down the shiny tin.

The other dolls followed his example and scooted along behind him.

When Raggedy Andy came to the place where he expected to find the penny dolls lying, they were nowhere about.

"Perhaps you scooted them farther than you thought!" Uncle Clem said.

22

"Perhaps I did!" Raggedy Andy said. "We will look around the bend in the eave!"

"Oh dear!" he exclaimed when he had peeped around the corner of the roof. "The gutter ends here and there is nothing but a hole!"

"They must have scooted right into the hole," the Dutch doll said.

Raggedy Andy lay flat upon the shiny tin and looked down into the hole.

"Are you down there, penny dolls?" he called.

There was no answer.

"I hope their heads were not broken!" Raggedy Ann said.

"I'm so sorry I scooted them!" Raggedy Andy cried, as he brushed his hand over his shoe-button eyes.

"Maybe if you hold my feet, I can reach down the hole and find them and pull them up again!" he added.

Uncle Clem and the Dutch doll each took hold of one of Raggedy Andy's feet and let him slide down into the hole.

It was a rather tight fit, but Raggedy Andy wiggled and

twisted until all the dolls could see of him were his two feet.

"I can't find them!" he said in muffled tones. "Let me down farther and I think I'll be able to reach them!"

Now the Dutch doll and Uncle Clem thought that Raggedy Andy meant for them to let go of his feet and this they did.

Raggedy Andy kept wiggling and twisting until he came to a bend in the pipe and could go no farther.

"I can't find them!" he cried. "They have gone farther down the pipe! Now you can pull me up!"

"We can't reach you, Raggedy Andy!" Uncle Clem called down the pipe. "Try to wiggle back up a bit and we will catch your feet and pull you up!"

Raggedy Andy tried to wiggle backward up the pipe, but his clothes caught upon a little piece of tin that stuck out from the inside of the pipe and there he stayed. He could neither go down nor come back up.

"What shall we do?" Uncle Clem cried. "The folks will never find him down there, for we cannot tell them where he is, and they will never guess it!"

The dolls were all very sad. They stayed up on the shiny new tin gutter until it began raining and hoped and hoped that Raggedy Andy could get back up to them.

Then they went inside the nursery and sat looking out the window until it was time for the folks to get up and the house to stir. Then they went back to the position each had been in when Marcella had left them.

And although they were very quiet, each one was so sorry to lose Raggedy Andy, and each felt that he would never be found again.

"The rain must have soaked his cotton through and through!" sighed Raggedy Ann. "For all the water from the house runs down the shiny tin gutters and down the pipe into a rain barrel at the bottom!"

Then Raggedy Ann remembered that there was an opening at the bottom of the pipe.

"Tomorrow night, if we have a chance, we must take a stick and see if we can reach Raggedy Andy from the bottom of the pipe and pull him down to us!" she thought.

Marcella came up to the nursery and played all day, watching the rain patter upon the new tin gutter. She wondered where Raggedy Andy was, although she did not get worried about him until she had asked Mama where he might be.

"He must be just where you left him!" Mama said.

"I cannot remember where I left him!" Marcella said.

"I thought he was with all the other dolls in the nursery, though!"

All day Sunday it rained and all of Sunday night, and Monday morning when Daddy started off to work it was still raining.

As Daddy walked out the front gate, he turned to wave good-bye to Mama and Marcella and then he saw something.

Daddy came right back into the house and called up the men who had put in the new shiny tin gutters.

"The drain pipe is plugged up. Some of you must have left shavings or something in the eaves, and it has washed down into the pipe, so that the water pours over the gutter in sheets!"

"We will send a man right up to fix it!" the men said.

So at about ten o'clock that morning one of the men came to fix the pipe.

But although he punched a long pole down the pipe, and punched and punched, he could not dislodge whatever it was that plugged the pipe and kept the water from running through it.

Then the man measured with his stick, so that he knew just where the place was, and with a pair of tin shears he cut

a section from the pipe and found Raggedy Andy.

Raggedy Andy was punched quite out of shape and all jammed together, but when the man straightened out the funny little figure, Raggedy Andy looked up at him with his customary happy smile.

The man laughed and carried little water-soaked Raggedy Andy into the house.

"I guess your little girl must have dropped this rag doll down into the drainpipe!" the man said to Mama.

"I'm so glad you found him!" Mama said to the man.

"We have hunted all over the house for him! Marcella could not remember where she put him, so when I get him nice and dry, I'll hide him in a nice easy place for her to find, and she will not know he has been out in the rain all night!"

So Mama put Raggedy Andy behind the radiator and there he sat all afternoon, steaming and drying out.

And as he sat there he smiled and smiled, even though there was no one to see him.

He felt very happy within and he always smiled, anyway, because his smile was painted on.

And another reason Raggedy Andy smiled was because he was not lonesome.

Inside his waist were the two little penny dolls.

The man had punched Raggedy Andy farther down into the pipe, and he had been able to reach the two little dolls and tuck them into a safe place.

"Won't they all be surprised to see us back again!" Raggedy Andy whispered as he patted the two little penny dolls with his soft rag hands.

And the two little penny dolls nestled against Raggedy Andy's soft cotton-stuffed body, and thought how nice it was to have such a happy, sunny friend.

Johnny Gruelle

DOCTOR RAGGEDY ANDY

RAGGEDY ANDY, Raggedy Ann, Uncle Clem and the Dutch doll were not given medicine because, you see, they had no mouths—that is, mouths through which medicine could be poured. Their mouths were either painted on, or were sewed on with yarn.

Sometimes the medicine spoon would be touched to their faces but none of the liquid would be given to them. Except accidentally.

But the French doll had a lovely mouth for taking medicine. It was open and showed her teeth in a dimpling smile. She also had soft brown eyes that opened and closed when she was tilted backward or forward.

The medicine that was given the dolls had great curing properties. It would cure the most stubborn case of croup, measles, whooping cough or any other ailment the dolls had wished upon them by their little mistress.

Some days all the dolls would be put to bed with measles, but in the course of half an hour they would have every other ailment in the doctor book.

The dolls enjoyed it very much, for, you see, Marcella always tried the medicine first to see if it was strong enough before she gave any to the dolls. So the dolls really did not get as much of the medicine as their little mistress.

The wonderful remedy was made from a very old recipe

handed down from ancient times. This recipe is guaranteed to cure every ill a doll may have. The medicine was made from brown sugar and water. Perhaps you may have used it for your dollies.

The medicine was also used as tea and soda water, except when the dolls were supposed to be ill.

Having nothing but painted or yarn mouths, the ailments of Raggedy Andy, Raggedy Ann, Uncle Clem and the Dutch doll mostly consisted of sprained wrists, arms and legs, or perhaps a headache and a toothache.

None of them knew they had the trouble until Marcella had wrapped up the injured rag arm, leg or head, and had explained in detail just what was the matter.

Raggedy Andy, Raggedy Ann, Uncle Clem or the Dutch doll were just as happy with their heads tied up for a toothache as they were without their heads tied up. Not having teeth, naturally they could not have a toothache, and if they could furnish amusement for Marcella by having her pretend they had a toothache, then that made them very happy.

So this day, the French doll was quite ill. She started out with the croup, and went through the measles, whooping cough and yellow fever in an hour.

The attack came on quite suddenly.

The French doll was sitting quietly in one of the little red chairs, smiling the prettiest of dimpling smiles at Raggedy Andy, and thinking of the romp the dolls would have that night after the house grew quiet when Marcella discovered that the French doll had the croup and put her to bed.

The French doll closed her eyes when put to bed, but the rest of her face did not change expression. She still wore her happy smile.

Marcella mixed very strong medicine and poured it into the French doll's open mouth.

She was given a dose every minute or so.

It was during the yellow fever stage that Marcella was called to supper and left the dolls in the nursery alone.

Marcella did not play with them again that evening, so the dolls all remained in the same positions until Marcella and the rest of the folks went to bed.

Then Raggedy Andy jumped from his chair and wound up the little music box. ''Let's start with a lively dance!'' he cried.

When the music started tinkling he caught the French doll's hand, and danced way across the nursery floor before he discovered that her soft brown eyes remained as closed as they were when she lay upon the sick bed.

All the dolls gathered around Raggedy Andy and the French doll.

"I can't open my eyes!" she said.

Raggedy Andy tried to open the French doll's eyes with his soft rag hands, but it was no use.

They shook her. This sometimes has the desired effect when dolls do not open their eyes.

They shook her again and again. It was no use! Her eyes remained closed.

"It must be the sticky, sugary medicine!" said Uncle Clem.

"I really believe it must be!" the French doll replied. "The medicine seemed to settle in the back of my head when I was lying down, and I can still feel it back there!"

"That must be it, and now it has hardened and keeps your pretty eyes from working!" said Raggedy Ann. "What shall we do?"

Raggedy Andy and Raggedy Ann walked over to a corner of the nursery and thought and thought. They pulled their foreheads down into wrinkles with their hands so that they might think harder.

Finally Raggedy Ann cried, "I've thought of a plan!" and went skipping from the corner out to where the other dolls sat around the French doll.

"We must stand her upon her head, then the medicine will run up into her hair, for there is a hole in the top of her head. I remember seeing it when her hair came off one time!"

"No sooner said than done!" cried Uncle Clem as he took the French doll by the waist and stood her upon her head.

"That should be long enough!" Raggedy Ann said,

when Uncle Clem had held the French doll in this position for about five minutes.

But when the French doll was again placed upon her feet her eyes still remained tightly closed.

All this time, Raggedy Andy had remained in the corner, thinking as hard as his rag head could think.

He thought and thought, until the yarn hair upon his head stood up in the air and wiggled.

"If the medicine did not run out into her hair when she stood upon her head," thought Raggedy Andy, "then it is because the medicine could not run, so, if the medicine cannot run, it is because it is too sticky and thick to run out the hole in the top of her head." He also thought a lot more.

At last he turned to the others and said out loud, "I can't seem to think of a single way to help her open her eyes unless we take off her hair and wash the medicine from inside her china head."

"Why didn't I think of that?" Raggedy Ann asked. "That is just what we shall have to do!"

So Raggedy Ann caught hold of the French doll's feet, and Raggedy Andy caught hold of the French doll's lively curls, and they pulled and they pulled.

Then the other dolls caught hold of Raggedy Ann and Raggedy Andy and pulled and pulled, until finally, with a sharp *"R-R-Rip!"* the French doll's hair came off, and the dolls who were pulling went tumbling over backward.

Laughingly they scrambled to their feet and sat the French doll up, so they might look into the hole in the top of her head.

Yes, the sticky medicine had grown hard and would not let the French doll's eyes open.

Raggedy Andy put his hand inside and pushed on the eyes so that they opened.

This was all right, only now the eyes would not close when the French doll lay down. She tried it.

So Raggedy Andy ran down into the kitchen and brought up a small tin cup full of warm water and a tiny rag.

With these he loosened the sticky medicine and washed the inside of the French doll's head nice and clean.

There were lots of cookie and cracker crumbs inside her head, too.

Raggedy Andy washed it all nice and clean, and then wet the glue, which made the pretty curls stay on.

So when her hair was placed upon her head again, the French doll was as good as new.

"Thank you all very much!" she said, as she tilted backward and forward, and found that her eyes worked very easily.

Raggedy Andy again wound up the little music box and, catching the French doll about the waist, started a rollicking dance that lasted until the roosters in the neighborhood began their morning crowing.

Then, knowing the folks might soon be stirring, the dolls left off their playing, and all took the same position they had been in when Marcella left them the night before.

And so Marcella found them.

The French doll was in bed with her eyes closed, and her happy dimpling smile lighting up her pretty face.

And to this day, the dollies' little mistress does not know that Raggedy Andy was the doctor who cured the French doll of her only illness.

MAKING "ANGELS" IN THE SNOW

"*WHEE!* It's good to be back home again!" said Raggedy Andy to the other dolls, as he stretched his feet out in front of the little toy stove and rubbed his rag hands briskly together, as if to warm them.

All the dolls laughed at Raggedy Andy for doing this, for they knew there had never been a fire in the little stove in all the time it had been in the nursery. And that was a long time.

"We are so glad and happy to have you back home again with us!" the dolls told Raggedy Andy. "For we have missed you very, very much!"

"Well," Raggedy Andy replied, as he held his rag hands over the tiny lid of the stove and rubbed them again, "I have missed all of you, too, and wished many times that you had been with me to join in and share in the pleasures and frolics I've had."

And as Raggedy Andy continued to hold his hands over the little stove, Uncle Clem asked him why he did it.

Raggedy Andy smiled and leaned back in his chair. "Really," he said, "I wasn't paying any attention to what I was doing! I've spent so much of my time while I was

away drying out my soft cotton stuffing it seems as though it has almost become a habit.''

''Were you wet most of the time, Raggedy Andy?'' the French doll asked.

''Nearly all the time!'' Raggedy Andy replied. ''First I would get sopping wet and then I'd freeze!''

''Freeze!'' exclaimed all the dolls in one breath.

''Dear me, yes!'' Raggedy Andy laughed. ''Just see here!'' And Raggedy Andy pulled his sleeve up and showed where his rag arm had been mended. ''That was quite a rip!'' he smiled.

''Dear! Dear! How in the world did it happen? On a nail?'' the Dutch doll asked as he put his arm about Raggedy Andy.

''Froze!'' said Raggedy Andy.

The dolls gathered around Raggedy Andy and examined the rip in his rag arm.

''It's all right now!'' he laughed. ''But you should have seen me when it happened! I was frozen into one solid cake of ice all the way through, and when Marcella tried to limber up my arm before it had thawed out, it went *'Pop!'* and just burst.

''Then I was placed in a pan of nice warm water until the icy cotton inside me had melted, and then I was hung up on a line above the kitchen stove, out at Grandma's.''

''But how did you happen to get so wet and then freeze?'' asked Raggedy Ann.

''Out across the road from Grandma's home, way out in the country, there is a lovely pond,'' Raggedy Andy explained. ''In the summertime pretty flowers grow about the edge, the little green frogs sit upon the pond lilies and beat upon their tiny drums all through the night and the twinkling stars wink at their reflections in the smooth water. But when Marcella and I went out to Grandma's, last week, Grandma met us with a sleigh, for the ground

was covered with starry snow. The pretty pond was covered with ice, too, and upon the ice was a soft blanket of the white, white snow. It was beautiful!'' said Raggedy Andy.

''Grandma had a lovely new sled for Marcella, a red one with shiny runners.

'' And after we had visited Grandma a while, we went to the pond for a slide.

''It was heaps of fun, for there was a little hill at one end of the pond so that when we coasted down, we went scooting across the pond like an arrow.

''Marcella would turn the sled sideways, just for fun, and she and I would fall off and go sliding across the ice upon our backs, leaving a clean path of ice, where we pushed aside the snow as we slid. Then Marcella showed me how to make 'angels' in the soft snow!''

''Oh, tell us how, Raggedy Andy!'' shouted all the dollies.

''It's very easy!'' said Raggedy Andy. ''Marcella would lie down upon her back in the snow and put her hands back up over her head, then she would bring her hands in a circle down to her sides, like this.'' And Raggedy Andy lay upon the floor of the nursery and showed the dollies just how it was done. "Then," he added, "when she stood up it would leave the print of her body and legs in the white, white snow, and where she had swooped, her arms there were the 'angel's wings!'"

"It must have looked just like an angel!" said Uncle Clem.

"Indeed it was very pretty!" Raggedy Andy answered. "Then Marcella made a lot of 'angels' by placing me in the snow and working my arms. So you see, what with falling off the sled so much and making so many 'angels,' we both were wet, but I was completely soaked through. My cotton just became soppy and I was ever so much heavier! Then Grandma, just as we were having a most delightful time, came to the door and *'Oooh-hooed'* to Marcella to come and get a nice new doughnut. So Marcella, thinking to return in a minute, left me lying upon the sled and ran through the snow to Grandma's. And there I stayed and stayed until I began to feel stiff and could hear the cotton inside me go, *'Tic! Tic!'* as it began to freeze.

"I lay upon the sled until after the sun went down. Two little chickadees came and sat upon the sled and talked to me in their cute little bird language, and I watched the sky in the west get golden red, then turn into a deep crimson purple and finally a deep blue, as the sun went farther down around the bend of the earth. After it had been dark for some time, I heard someone coming through the snow and could see the yellow light of a lantern. It was Grandma.

"She pulled the sled over in back of her house and did not see that I was upon it until she turned to go in the kitchen. Then she picked me up and took me inside. 'He's frozen stiff as a board!' she told Marcella as she handed

47

me to her.   Marcella did not say why she had forgotten to come for me, but I found out afterward that it was because she was so wet.   Grandma made her change her clothes and shoes and stockings and would not permit her to go out and play again.

"Well, anyway," concluded Raggedy Andy, "Marcella tried to limber my arm and, being almost solid ice, it just burst.   And that is the way it went all the time we were out at Grandma's.   I was wet nearly all the time.   But I wish you could all have been with me to share in the fun."

And Raggedy Andy again leaned over the little toy stove and rubbed his rag hands briskly together.

Uncle Clem went to the waste basket and came back with some scraps of yellow and red paper.   Then, taking off one of the tiny lids, he stuffed the paper in part of the way as if the flames were shooting up!

Then, as all the dolls' merry laughter rang out, Raggedy Andy stopped rubbing his hands, and catching Raggedy Ann about the waist, he went skipping across the nursery floor with her, whirling so fast neither saw they had gone out through the door until it was too late.   For coming to the head of the stairs, they both went head over heels, *"Blumpity, blump!"* over and over, until they wound up, laughing, at the bottom.

"Last one up is a rotten egg!" cried Raggedy Ann, as she scrambled to her feet.   And with her skirts in her rag hands she went racing up the stairs to where the rest of the dollies stood laughing.

"Hurray, for Raggedy Ann!" cried Raggedy Andy generously.   "She won!"

THE SINGING SHELL

FOR YEARS and years the beautiful shell had been upon the floor in Grandma's front room. It was a large shell with many points on it. These were coarse and rough, but the shell was most beautiful inside.

Marcella had seen the shell time and time again and often admired its lovely coloring, which could be seen when one looked inside the shell.

So one day, Grandma gave the beautiful shell to Marcella to have for her very own, up in the nursery.

"It will be nice to place before the nursery door so the wind will not blow the door closed and pinch anyone's fingers!" Grandma laughed.

So Marcella brought the shell home and placed it in front of the nursery door. Here the dolls saw it that night, when all the house was still, and stood about it wondering what kind of toy it might be.

"It seems to be nearly all mouth!" said the Dutch doll. "Perhaps it can talk."

"It has teeth!" the French doll pointed out. "It may bite!"

"I do not believe it will bite," Raggedy Andy mused, as he got down upon his hands and knees and looked up into the shell. "Marcella would not have it up here if it would bite!" And, saying this, Raggedy Andy put his rag arm into the lovely shell's mouth.

49

"It doesn't bite! I knew it wouldn't!" he cried. "Just feel how smooth it is inside!"

All the dolls felt and were surprised to find it polished so smoothly inside, while the outside was so coarse and rough. With the help of Uncle Clem and the Dutch doll, Raggedy Andy turned the shell upon its back, so that all the dolls might look in.

The coloring consisted of dainty pinks, creamy whites and pale blues, all running together just as the coloring in an opal runs from one shade into another. Raggedy Andy, stooping over to look farther up inside the pretty shell, heard something.

"It's whispering!" he said, as he raised up in surprise.

All the dolls took turns putting their ears to the mouth of the beautiful shell. Yes, truly it whispered, but they could not catch just what it said.

Finally Raggedy Andy suggested that all the dolls lie down upon the floor directly in front of the shell and keep very quiet.

"If we don't make a sound we may be able to hear what it says!" he explained.

So the dolls lay down, placing themselves flat upon the floor directly in front of the shell and where they could see and admire its beautiful coloring.

Now the dolls could be very, very quiet when they really wished to be, and it was easy for them to hear the faint whispering of the shell.

This is the story the shell told the dolls in the nursery that night:

"A long, long time ago, I lived upon the yellow sand, deep down beneath the blue, blue waters of the ocean. Pretty silken weeds grew up around my home and reached their waving branches up, up toward the top of the water.

"Through the pretty seaweed, fishes of pretty colors and shapes darted here and there, playing their games.

"It was still and quiet way down where I lived, for
even if the ocean roared and pounded itself into an angry
mass of tumbling waves up above, this never disturbed the
calm waters down where I lived.

"Many times, little fishes or other tiny sea people came
and hid within my pretty house when they were being
pursued by larger sea creatures. And it always made me
very happy to give them this protection.

"They would stay inside until I whispered that the
larger creature had gone, then they would leave me and
return to their play.

"Pretty little sea horses with slender, curving bodies
often went sailing above me, or would come to rest upon my
back. It was nice to lie and watch the tiny things curl their
little tails about the seaweed and talk together, for the sea
horses like one another and are gentle and kind to each other,

52

sharing their food happily and smoothing their little ones with their cunning noses.

"But one day a diver leaped over the side of a boat and came swimming head first down, down to where I lay. My! How the tiny sea creatures scurried to hide from him. He took me in his hand and, giving his feet a thump upon the yellow sand, rose with me to the surface.

"He poured the water from me, and out came all the little creatures who had been hiding there!"

Raggedy Andy wiggled upon the floor, he was so interested.

"Did the tiny creatures get back into the water safely?" he asked the beautiful shell.

"Oh, yes!" the shell whispered in reply. "The man held me over the side of the boat, so the tiny creatures went safely back into the water!"

"I am so glad!" Raggedy Andy said, with a sigh of relief. "He must have been a kindly man!"

"Yes, indeed!" the beautiful shell replied. "So I was placed along with a lot of other shells in the bottom of the boat and every once in a while another shell was placed among us. We whispered together and wondered where we were going. We were finally sold to different people and I have been at Grandma's house for a long, long time."

"You lived there when Grandma was a little girl, didn't you?" Raggedy Ann asked.

"Yes," replied the shell, "I have lived there ever since Grandma was a little girl. She often used to play with me and listen to me sing."

"Raggedy Ann can play 'Peter, Peter, Pumpkin Eater' on the piano with one hand," said Uncle Clem, "but none of us can sing. Will you sing for us?" he asked the shell.

"I sing all the time," the shell replied, "for I cannot help singing, but my singing is a secret and so it is very soft

53

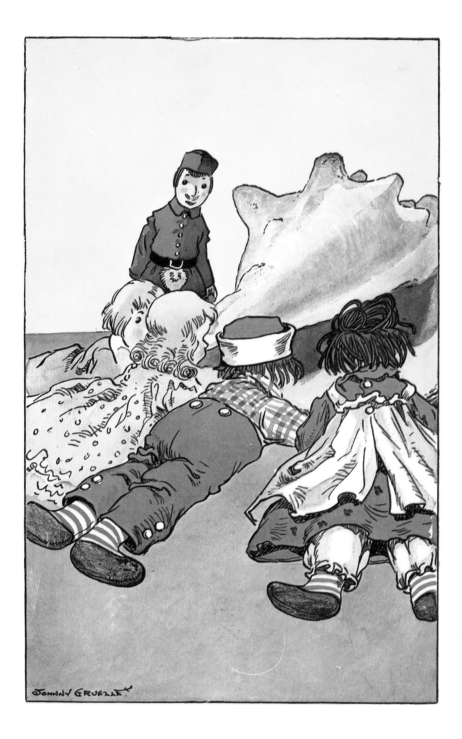

and low. Put your head close to the opening in my shell and listen!"

The dolls took turns doing this, and heard the shell sing softly and very sweetly.

"How strange and far away it sounds!" exclaimed the French doll. "Like Fairies singing in the distance! The shell must be singing the songs of the Mermaids and the Water Fairies!"

"It is strange that anything so rough on the outside could be so pretty within!" said Raggedy Andy. "It must be a great pleasure to be able to sing so sweetly!"

"Indeed it is," replied the beautiful shell, "and I get great happiness from singing all the time."

"And you will bring lots of pleasure to us, by being so happy!" said Raggedy Andy. "For although you may not enter into our games, we will always know that you are happily singing, and that will make us all happy!"

"I will tell you the secret of my singing," said the shell. "When anyone puts an ear to me and listens, he or she hears the reflection of one's own heart's music, singing. So you see, while I say that I am singing all the time, in reality I sing only when someone full of happiness hears one's own singing as if it were mine."

"How unselfish you are to say this!" said Raggedy Andy. "Now we are ever so much more glad to have you with us. Aren't we?" he asked, turning to the rest of the dolls.

"Yes, indeed!" came the answer from all the dolls, even the tiny penny dolls.

"That is why the shell is so beautiful inside!" said Raggedy Ann. "Those who are unselfish may wear rough clothes, but inside they are always beautiful, just like the shell, and reflect to others the happiness and sunny music within their hearts!"